COLONY OF FEAR

AN AMERICAN FAMILY™ BOOK ONE: 1692

Colony of Fear

LUCY JANE BLEDSOE

NR
FICTION
B1

FEARON EDUCATION
a division of
David S. Lake Publishers
Belmont, California

Cover illustrator: Terry Hoff

ISBN 0-8224-4751-7

Library of Congress Catalog Card Number: 88-81520

Printed in the United States of America

1. 9 8 7 6 5 4 3 2 1

FAMILY TREE

Samuel Roberts (1672–1728)
married
Anne Rockmore (1674–1730)

AN AMERICAN FAMILY™ SERIES

Contents

The Gallows

Samuel Roberts lay curled up in a tiny prison cell. The cell was so dark, he couldn't see his own hand. The stone walls were as cold as ice. And the floor was nothing but damp soil. The cold blackness chilled Samuel to the bone.

Samuel desperately wanted to sleep. But as he lay there, he felt a small creature crawl across his throat. He jumped to his feet, and cracked his head on the stone ceiling.

"Oooooh," he groaned. His six-foot figure crumbled into a ball on the floor. This prison cell seemed to be full of creatures. All night Samuel could hear their scratching and slithering. Another 24 hours in this cell and he'd go mad.

"No," Samuel said out loud to himself. "You've got to hold onto your senses—"

He stopped when he heard two men's voices in the hall. Then the flickering light of a candle cast a small shadow on his cell wall.

"Did you hear that?" one of the approaching men said. "He was talking to himself. Oh, a sure sign, a sure sign."

"I won't touch him," said the other man. "I have a wife and children."

"But you're a bigger man than I," the first voice whined. "Your soul can head off the powers of darkness. With my luck, should I touch the man once, the Devil will leap into my heart in a minute."

The two men stopped outside Samuel's cell. The first voice hissed, "I say he should hang today! Before Satan grips Stonesbury as he has Salem."

Samuel pounded his fist on the bars. "Let me out of here, you fools! Take me to my trial! I'd no more run from the chance to speak to the townspeople of Stonesbury than I'd run from the Devil himself." The men gasped. "Open the door!" Samuel said.

He heard a hasty jangling of keys. Then his cell door swung open and the two guards leapt back.

"Boo!" Samuel shouted. The men nearly jumped out of their skins. Samuel laughed harshly. "Fools," he mumbled.

The prison hall was dimly lit, but at least Samuel could see again. The two guards scurried ahead of him like mice. Though not quite 21 years old, Samuel was the tallest man in Stonesbury. He had to duck as he made his way down the hall.

Stepping out into the bright June sunshine, Samuel scowled. The sudden brightness hurt his eyes.

Samuel looked out over the town in which he'd lived for almost four years. Stonesbury, 50 miles inland from Boston, was surrounded by farms and forests. The town was made up of a few shops, a few homes, the tavern and the inn. The best location, next door to the meetinghouse, was the Reverend Rockmore's two-story home. In the center of town was the grassy field the townspeople called the commons.

Today, several men were at work in the commons. Samuel stared at them. Horror filled his entire being.

The men had built a 20-foot wooden structure. Some of the men were on top of it hammering pegs into the crossbeam. Others stood below steadying the two upright beams. These men were building a gallows.

"Madness!" Samuel cried. "Madness has seized Massachusetts!"

"Not madness," one of the guards answered. "The Devil."

As the guards marched Samuel down the street, he clutched his throat. He knew the gallows were being built just for him. A moment later he stood before the meeting-house where his trial would take place. Only then did Samuel forget his own neck. For now he could see Anne Rockmore standing in the pillory. Her hands and head dangled from the holes cut in the locked wooden structure. The woman's dark hair had been loosened to shame her, and it hung over her face.

"Anne," Samuel whispered. His heart ached as he looked at her. He reached out to brush back her tangle of hair. But a guard's club swung down on his hand. Samuel cried out in pain.

Anne turned her head up as best she could. Though her face was bathed in sweat, her eyes were clear. She wrenched her mouth into a painful smile and spoke. "Samuel, remember that I love you."

"Get moving!" the guard growled, pushing Samuel forward. But Anne's smile, and her words, had already given him strength. He stepped proudly into the meetinghouse to face the charges of witchcraft.

As he entered the room, Samuel saw that everyone in town had come to witness his trial. They all seemed eager for his hanging. Nausea gripped Samuel's stomach. His knees weakened, and he began to feel very light-headed. A moment later, Samuel slumped to the floor.

And in that moment, memories passed through his mind as if he were a man on the edge of death.

First Years in America

In 1684, a boy of 12 stood on the deck of a large ship. As he grasped the railing, he stared into the Atlantic Ocean. For months the rocking of the ship had caused him to feel dizzy and nauseous. Even so, Samuel was happy. He and his parents were going to America. Soon they would be living in a land where gold nuggets lined river streams like ordinary rocks.

"You know those stories of gold are not really true," his mother had said on their first day at sea. "We are going to America to live in the Quaker settlement William Penn began. There we will be able to worship freely. But don't expect it to be easy, my boy."

Her words fell on deaf ears. The 12-year-old fully expected to make his fortune in America.

However, Samuel's dreams were soon cruelly dashed. One month after landing in America, Samuel's mother and infant sister died in childbirth. And his father, who had taken sick on the voyage, never recovered. He died just two weeks later.

Samuel was taken in by a kind farmer and his family who lived outside of Philadelphia. For four years Samuel worked hard alongside the farmer's six sons. He felt very proud to be a member of this unusual American community. The Quakers believed that everyone should be allowed to worship as they pleased. Also, every man had the right to vote in Pennyslvania Colony. It didn't matter what his beliefs were, or whether or not he had money. Things were not the same, Samuel was told, in other American colonies.

But Samuel still had dreams about a new kind of life. He'd already lived on a farm in England. He expected something different in America.

When Samuel was 16 years old, he read a flyer posted in the Philadelphia Inn. "Wanted," the flyer read. "A hardworking shoemaker's apprentice. Four-year service. All standard conditions apply. See Master Bacon, Stonesbury, Massachusetts."

That very night Samuel explained to the farmer that he planned to apply for the position. The man's six sons looked on, wide-eyed.

"But what if you do not get the position?" the farmer asked. "And how will you even get to Stonesbury? Where will you sleep? And what about food? My son, the Puritans are good hardworking people. But they are very different from our Quakers. Samuel, the Puritans have hung more than one Quaker just for having different religious beliefs. How can you know that you will be welcome there?"

But Samuel had already made up his mind. The following morning he was on the road to Massachusetts. The boy had only the clothes on his back and a sack of biscuits made by the farmer's wife. If he had had a horse, the trip to Stonesbury would have taken three weeks. Instead, Samuel was forced to walk. He stopped along the way to work for his meals and his lodging. So, he didn't arrive in Stonesbury for six weeks. By then it was late in November, and the weather was cold.

Shivering and very hungry, Samuel found an inn. "Sir? May I offer my services at anything for the price of a bed and dinner?" he asked the innkeeper.

"Ho! No!" the man shouted. "What do you think this is? Suppose I took in every dirty, wayward child of the road. Do you think I could pay for my cider and ale? Move along, boy!"

"I can do a man's work!" Samuel answered, as he backed out of the inn. He cursed his own childish face, which was still soft and round. His shoulders, too, were still childishly narrow. But Samuel was strong. And his huge hands and feet promised further growth soon.

Samuel stood in the commons as dusk gathered around the town of Stonesbury. His eyes caught the stocks and pillory in front of the meetinghouse. A boy about his age sat locked in the stocks. Samuel had heard talk of such New England practices. But he hadn't believed they were true. Now the sight of a person in such a situation gave him a sick feeling. He turned around and hurried out of town as a light snow began to fall.

Samuel made his way back to a stream he'd noticed earlier. By the side of the road he tore pine boughs off some trees. He used some of them for a bed. The others he piled on top of himself. Cold through to the bone, and just as hungry, Samuel fell into a restless sleep.

At daybreak, he woke under a light blanket of snow. He washed as best as he could in the stream. Then, he set a quick pace into town to warm up.

The first shop in town was the general store. Samuel stopped there to ask directions to the shoemaker's. A fire blazed in the back room. Samuel breathed in the warm, spicy smells. The firelight brightened the barrels of crackers, pickles, and candy. Along the walls were pitchforks and horsewhips. A handsome young man, a few years older than Samuel, was dusting.

"Help you?"

"Uh," Samuel's voice cracked. He lowered it and went on. "I'm looking for Master Bacon, the shoemaker. I've, uh, come to apply for the apprenticeship."

The young man looked Samuel over and shook his head. "Why don't you come on back to the house with me? Have some breakfast and a wash before you apply to Master Bacon."

"I've come only for directions—" Samuel started. His ears burned with embarrassment. He knew that his bones pushed out from his flesh. After all, he'd been walking for six weeks with very little to eat. But did he look that bad?

"I'm Nathaniel," the young man continued. "You can borrow a clean shirt, too. It might help."

In the house behind the store Samuel met Nathaniel's family. The crackling of a rabbit roasting over the fire made Samuel shake with hunger. Nathaniel's mother saw Samuel's eyes staring at the meat. Though it was hours before dinner, she cut a fat slice off the rabbit. Then she spooned a heap of corn pudding next to the meat and served everything on a plate. The woman smiled as Samuel quickly dug his fork into the food.

Samuel didn't understand these Puritans. One denies a hungry boy a bite in exchange for work. The next one offers him dinner and clean clothing for nothing.

"What skills have you?" asked Nathaniel. Samuel remained silent. "Ah," continued the older boy, "you look as if you will grow strong soon. You'll make a good match for Susannah." Nathaniel winked, and then laughed at Samuel's puzzled look. "The shoemaker's daughter, of course. She is part of the deal, you know. If you get the job, and do it well, that is. Where are you from?"

"Philadelphia."

"A Quaker?" asked Nathaniel.

Samuel nodded.

"A good people. But go carefully," Nathaniel warned. "The Quakers are none too popular in Massachusetts. But you must already know that. I say you and I may have something in common. Politically, that is."

Samuel, wary of this talkative young man, said little. But when Nathaniel tossed him a clean shirt, Samuel smiled. "Just return it when you can," Nathaniel said. Samuel thanked him and his mother. Then he made his way across the commons to see Master Bacon.

The cobbler's shop was very clean. Spools of waxed thread were lined up neatly on a table. Cowhides were stretched before a fire. A man with a large belly and curly gray hair sat bent over a boot. He yanked a hog's bristle needle through the leather and pulled the thread.

"What do you want, son?" the cobbler asked without looking up.

"I've come to apply for Master Bacon's apprenticeship."

The man looked up, startled. "You're not from Stonesbury. How did you hear so fast?"

"Sir. I read the flyer in Philadelphia six weeks ago."

"Oh!" the shoemaker laughed. "That position was filled about four weeks ago."

Samuel bit his lip, his heart sinking.

"How did you come from Philadelphia?"

"I walked, sir."

The shoemaker put down his work and studied Samuel. He looked hard into the boy's eyes. Then he slowly examined the rest of him.

"You might be in luck, boy. Look out the window toward the meetinghouse. That's what became of the fellow I hired four weeks ago."

Samuel turned and looked at the boy in the stocks.

"Too fond of his cider, that boy. I let him go yesterday and he quickly got into trouble." He paused, and then went on. "Well, sit down and I'll talk to you, anyway. Philadelphia, you say. Quaker?"

The master's eyes narrowed. He leaned forward. Samuel knew his answer could cost him the job.

"Yes, sir. But I am not here to change anyone's ways, sir."

"Ah, yes." The man looked thoughtful. "But you see Stonesbury would not look too kindly on my hiring a Quaker. I am second in command on the town council, you see. My brother-in-law, the Reverend Rockmore, is Stonesbury's leading preacher. Of course he is head of the town council as well." Bacon patted his stomach proudly. "You see, it would never do for me to hire a Quaker."

"Sir, I'd like a fair chance," Samuel said.

The master considered the boy's words, as if he'd never heard such a statement. "Mmm, fair chance," he mumbled. He looked around at the piles of shoes. He was already far behind in his work.

Then, speaking sharply, he said, "I run a tight ship here. Work from sunup to sundown. A four-year apprenticeship. No visits to the tavern, no courting, no marriage. An attic room with my younger children. Shoemaking is exacting and hard work. Do you still want a fair chance, boy? Or do you think perhaps—"

"Yes, sir," Samuel interrupted.

The cobbler leaned back, and rested his hands on his apron. His eyes narrowed once again.

"Listen carefully, then," Bacon said finally. "I would never, under most conditions, take on a Quaker. But my business is very good right now. With the snow setting in, everyone is wearing shoes again. Frankly, I'm in a tight place. Having lost my apprentice, I'm nearly desperate for help. I don't have time to advertise again. You're a very lucky boy. But remember, I will be strict. One slip, and you're out."

Samuel listened silently as the shoemaker spoke. "On the other hand, I am not an unfair man. Serve me with loyal, skilled, hard work, for four years. If you do, I shall give you the tools you need to begin your own shop. In another town, of course. Are you willing?"

Samuel smiled widely and said, "Yes, sir. Thank you very much, sir."

For the next three and a half years, Samuel proved to be an ideal apprentice. Because he was an outsider, and a Quaker, he knew he had to perform better than a local boy. Samuel worked harder and kept quieter than other boys his age. And he dutifully attended the Puritan church each week with his master's family.

By the time he was 20 years old, Samuel had grown to a full six feet. He towered over most of the other men in Stonesbury. His voice deepened, and he grew a reddish beard, just a shade lighter than his hair. His green eyes grew brighter each year from happiness and experience. He'd even taken on a jaunty, self-assured way of walking.

"Don't be too certain of yourself," Master Bacon warned. But Samuel knew his master was very satisfied with his services. Indeed, more than satisfied. In the spring of 1692, Bacon sat Samuel down and offered him more than Samuel had ever dreamed.

"Since I have five daughters and no sons," Bacon explained, "I have two problems. One is my business. The other is marrying off five girls. I was hoping I could use you to help solve both problems."

The master did more than offer his oldest daughter Susannah in marriage. He also proposed that Samuel join him in equal partnership. The business had grown quickly and the two men would hire a new apprentice. Without hesitation, Samuel agreed.

"One more thing," the cobbler told Samuel. "Let me speak plainly. I think everyone in Stonesbury has nearly forgotten that you are Quaker. Everyone, that is, except for my brother-in-law, Reverend Rockmore. Samuel, my brother-in-law doesn't like you. He thinks you are, well, a bit more self-assured than you should be. He warned me against marrying my Susannah to you. But as I have said, I do have five daughters to marry. I simply cannot afford to satisfy everyone.

"Besides, while I agree with my brother-in-law on most things, on this I do not. For three and a half years, I have known you to be a very honest and hardworking young man. To be sure, I have come to think of you as the son I never had.

"You must, of course, join the Puritan church before the marriage. But that is a small matter, now, isn't it?"

A Late-Night Meeting

Samuel lay in his attic bed and listened carefully. Finally, he heard the town crier's footsteps on the cobblestone street below. "Ten o'clock and all is well," Simon Weatherby shouted. Next, Samuel knew that Weatherby would pass under the attic window. Then he would circle the commons and step inside the inn to warm his hands. Samuel counted to one hundred and then crept out of bed. Looking out the window, he saw the back of Weatherby's jacket disappear inside the inn.

Perfect timing as usual, Samuel thought. He slipped his hand under the bed and pulled out a book. Then he climbed silently out of the small attic window. He grabbed a big branch of the oak, cursing the ice that still coated the tree. Hoping his hands would hold, Samuel swung out and grasped the trunk with his legs. Then he slid down the icy tree.

Samuel simply couldn't sleep as much as the rest of the Bacon family. Lately he was even more full of energy. Certainly these nighttime walks he took were harmless enough. But Samuel knew the Puritan town leaders, including his master, would not approve of them. Sometimes, Samuel just walked around the commons. But often, like tonight, he visited Nathaniel.

"Samuel! Good to see you, friend," Nathaniel said to Samuel when he knocked on his door. "Come warm yourself by the fire."

"I've almost finished your John Locke book," Samuel said brightly.

"Yes, and what do you think?" Nathaniel asked.

"What a thinker! Religious liberty is the Quaker belief, you know. And that every person has the right to life, health, liberty, and possessions sounds good to me."

"You read well," smiled Nathaniel. "I hope more men in Massachusetts read Locke. Did you hear the news, Samuel?"

"There's been so much. Of which news do you speak?"

"Three more so-called 'witches' were hung in Salem. I'm afraid this madness will not end for a while. The town council in Stonesbury seems to be thirsty for its own witch hunt."

"It is true," Samuel sighed. "The master speaks of witches at every meal."

"The leading preachers in Boston have called for a demon search throughout all of Massachusetts," Nathaniel continued. "The Reverend Rockmore will feel he has to deliver at least one witch to prove his purity."

"Do you really think so?" Samuel asked.

"I do, Samuel. And you know that the King's new charter for Massachusetts Colony threatens the Puritan stronghold on government. A witch hunt may be just the thing to rid Stonesbury of men supporting the Royal Charter."

"Nathaniel, you always think the worst of people," Samuel said.

"Listen, you know what the new Royal Charter says," Nathaniel replied. "All men who own property may vote, no matter what their religious beliefs. And Rockmore's town council has ignored the new charter for almost a year."

"But, believe me, Rockmore has felt the squeeze on his power," Nathaniel continued. "It has made him angry. And he is going to be even angrier. Wait until he learns that I have organized a Charter Committee. We are Stonesbury's freeholders who are not Puritan church members. Soon, we will hold a public meeting. We plan to force the King's law upon the Puritan church. We shall be voting members of this town if it's the last thing we do."

"I shall back you all the way!" Samuel said.

"No!" Nathaniel said firmly. "I suggest that you do not back us, publicly anyway. Samuel, your Quaker background puts you in much greater danger than the rest of us. Keep quiet. You will be a voter soon enough, as it is. Will you not be joining the church before marrying Susannah?" Nathaniel's voice broke on speaking Susannah's name. His face twisted as if he were controlling some emotion.

"Well, that is part of the arrangement."

"Yes, of course. So you need not get involved with the Charter Committee."

"But it's the principle of it!" cried Samuel, his face reddening. "Why did you give me Locke to read? Don't you believe his words are to be put into action?"

"You must beware of Rockmore," Nathaniel said.

"I'm not afraid of Rockmore, that old bag of wind," Samuel replied. "I've been an ideal apprentice," he added proudly. "I have nothing to fear. My master is a leading church member. He will protect me."

"Do you really believe your master would go against his own brother-in-law to stand by your side?"

"Why, he already has! The Reverend opposes my marriage to Susannah. But that has not stopped my master."

"Next to the charter, your marriage is a small thing," Nathaniel replied. He sounded almost angry.

Nathaniel calmed himself and continued. "Samuel, I have planned each of my political moves carefully. Do not throw yourself headlong into these affairs. You are a smart man. But you often act before you think. Be careful."

Nathaniel saw by the blank look in Samuel's eyes that he had stopped listening. Nathaniel then sighed and said, "Well, enough of that. Now tell me, are you happy with your upcoming marriage?"

"Couldn't be happier!" Samuel beamed. "Susannah will make a fine partner. And I can't complain about the dowry—half of a shoemaking business. What more could I ask?"

"You don't mind joining the church?"

"Ah, that. A small matter," Samuel replied, quoting his master's words.

"But you must publicly explain your conversion."

Samuel shrugged. He didn't want to think about that until he had to. He changed the subject. "Mind if I keep the Locke book a few more weeks?" he asked.

"Not at all," answered Nathaniel. With that, Samuel said good night and left.

The Reverend's Daughter

The following evening, Samuel did not visit Nathaniel again. Their talk the night before had left a bad taste in his mouth. Doubt, or perhaps fear, lapped at the edges of his thoughts.

What he had told Nathaniel was true: he couldn't be happier. Susannah, the business, what else was there? Yet something didn't quite fit. Perhaps it was this town. The people's growing concern with witches frightened Samuel. But surely Stonesbury would not start hanging people as they were doing in Salem.

Tonight Samuel slid down the oak tree and began walking around the outskirts of town. Before he knew it, he was standing in the woods directly behind the Reverend Rockmore's house.

Suddenly frightened, Samuel stopped and looked about the forest. A huge moon had risen. Next to deep black shadows were bright silvery patches of moonlight. Snow dropped softly from the trees.

Out of the corner of his eye, Samuel thought he saw something move. Next he heard footsteps. Then, straight ahead some 50 yards away, he saw her. It was a figure dancing round and round through a patch of moonlight. The woman's apron swirled, and her long dark pigtail swung about her face.

Samuel hid behind a tree. Witches, indeed! His heart jumped into his throat. The dancing woman moved in and out of the forest shadows. Each time she appeared, she was closer. Samuel wanted to run away. But if he moved, she might hear him. Yet if he didn't, she might discover him.

The figure moved into a nearby spot of moonlight. She stopped as suddenly and gracefully as a cat. She looked around, frightened.

Samuel caught his breath. It was the Reverend Rockmore's 18-year-old daughter!

Samuel began edging backward, one step at a time. Suddenly something cold and hard smacked him on the head. "Ahh!" he yelled, as he wiped the fallen snow off himself. The woman heard his yell and looked right at him. In horror, Samuel stared back.

"What are you doing?" Anne Rockmore finally demanded.

"I, uh, was just out walking," Samuel stammered.

The woman stood perfectly still and eyed Samuel. "You're my uncle's apprentice," she finally said.

"Yes, that is true. And you're the Reverend's daughter, Anne." Samuel searched his mind for something else to say. "I, uh, recognized those dancing steps," he finally blurted out. "I remember them from my childhood in England."

"I learned them from my mother," the woman answered.

Samuel's eyes widened. "The well-kept secrets of Puritan clergy!" he thought. "The wife of the Reverend Rockmore—a dancer!"

"I see," Samuel said after a moment. "I thought that the only dance master in

Massachusetts was driven out of Boston a few years ago."

"Yes, it is true," Anne replied. She took several bold steps toward him. "My window faces yours across the commons. I've watched you go out at night." Her dark eyes flashed in the moonlight. She seemed filled with a quiet confidence. Samuel took a step back. She continued, "I've mentioned this to no one."

"Ah!" Samuel smiled, now understanding. "This is blackmail. If I report *your* nighttime activities, you shall report mine in return. Am I right?"

Now Anne looked sheepish.

"Don't be afraid," Samuel said. "You know, there are so many rules in this town. I daresay a good many people must have a secret night life. As a child in England, I loved to wander at night. It is the one practice I've not been able to change for New England."

Anne smiled now, and seemed to relax.

"May I ask how it was your father permitted your mother to teach you to dance?"

"Oh, he never knew," Anne said. "Of course my father would never allow it. But dancing was a passion of my mother's. Before she died, Mother and I enjoyed many good times together."

"And when did she die?"

"Four years ago, when I was fourteen," Anne replied. "She was never strong. I believe Father's strictness got the best of her . . ." Her voice trailed off in sadness.

"And you? Will his strictness get the best of you?" Samuel asked.

"No," Anne said, speaking forcefully once more. "I'm much stronger than my mother."

Samuel nodded and smiled slightly. "Well, I should be getting home," he said.

"I see you have a book in your hand," Anne said. She seemed anxious to continue the conversation. "Do you read often?" she asked.

"As often as I can get hold of a book," Samuel answered.

"Father says books are the Devil's tools for wrenching the law from God's hands. Except for the Bible, of course."

"He must be worried about the men who want to enforce the King's new charter."

"He is."

"Yes, well, I think we've talked too much. I must—"

"I like to read, too," Anne went on. "I promise I will not breathe a word to anyone if you—"

Now Samuel interrupted. "Speak plainly to whomever you please! I have no secrets."

"That's not wise in this town," Anne warned.

Samuel shrugged.

"Do you think it possible for me to borrow your book?" Anne asked.

"Certainly not. The book is not mine to lend. And besides, what would your father say if he found it? I'd be on the whipping post for sure. Good night."

Rockmore's Warning

On Sunday morning, Samuel sat directly behind Anne Rockmore in the meetinghouse. Reverend Rockmore had now begun his third hour of preaching. But Samuel was not bored. He studied the dark curls that fell from Anne's cap. Once she turned her head a little. Then he could see her long eyelashes and the curve of her cheek.

Several seats down from Anne sat Susannah. Time and again, Samuel directed his attention toward his future wife. Susannah seemed as pale and lifeless as a rag doll. Her only movements came as she fidgeted in her seat. She was forever reaching up to her cap to check for stray hairs. Samuel couldn't help turning to watch Anne once again.

"Wrestle the Devil from your souls!" shouted Rockmore. Samuel was shocked to attention in his seat. The preacher leaned very far over the pulpit as he spoke. He looked as if he might fall into the congregation. His eyebrows, arched in a terrible scowl, looked like great overgrown bushes.

Rockmore continued preaching. "Three more witches were hanged this week in Salem, thank the Lord. Oh, citizens of Stonesbury, the Devil is not satisfied with Salem. Oh, no! He seeks soldiers throughout Massachusetts. In fact, in this very meetinghouse, there is someone flirting with the powers of darkness."

The Reverend stopped preaching. He began a slow, steady search through the congregation. His gaze landed on Samuel and stopped. Rockmore's eyes focused directly on him. Samuel felt his backbone turn to ice.

"Yes, the Devil has formed a committee in Stonesbury," Rockmore continued. He held his eyes on Samuel and kept his gravely voice very low. "He has convinced men that *they* have a right to rule Stonesbury. But I ask you a question this morning. What are the laws of a man, even the King of England, next to the law of God? Nothing but dust! God's charter is the only charter that rules Massachusetts."

That night Samuel sneaked out of the attic window again. Then he went to visit Nathaniel.

"I do not know if you should continue with your Charter Committee," Samuel told him. "You were right about Rockmore. Today in church he as much as said that the men backing the charter will be tried as witches."

"Yes, I know." Nathaniel was thoughtful. "If only I had a printing press! I could make copies of the charter so everyone could read it. Samuel, I know that at least half of this town would support us if they saw the charter in print."

"Some day you will have your press, my friend," Samuel said.

"But we need it *now*," Nathaniel insisted. "Things are changing quickly here. We must see that the change goes in the right direction."

Samuel nodded. "I agree. But you have to be careful. And now, I must return home."

When Samuel reached the oak tree below his window, he realized he'd forgotten to return the Locke book. That had been the main purpose of his visit to Nathaniel. Now he held the book with his teeth as he began climbing.

"Stalking Stonesbury at night, are you?" a voice hissed. Then Samuel felt a hand grab his foot. He looked down and saw the sneering face of Reverend Rockmore.

Rockmore yanked Samuel out of the tree. He snatched the book from his mouth. "John Locke! Religious liberty, indeed! Big ideas for a shoemaker's apprentice, don't you think, Roberts?"

Samuel's mouth felt like sand. He reached for the book, but Rockmore put it behind his back.

"You've gotten pretty big for your breeches, boy. Don't think I haven't seen that scornful look on you in church. John Locke, indeed. You are fortunate to be working for my dear late wife's brother. Otherwise you would never have lasted in my town. I told him not to hire a Quaker!"

Rockmore tossed the book in the mud. "Consider yourself warned, Roberts."

The next day Master Bacon's face showed a mixture of anger and worry. "Whatever for, Samuel?"

"I was going to the outhouse, sir," Samuel lied.

"By climbing out the attic window?"

"I didn't want to wake the family."

Master Bacon nodded doubtfully. "The Reverend Rockmore says you had with you a book by Locke."

Samuel looked at his feet and didn't speak.

"Bear in mind, my boy, that a lot rests on your behavior. I suggest you plan to join the church very soon."

The month of June brought more trouble. Witches were tried in Salem every day. Some were hanged. Others were thrown in prison. One man was crushed to death by stones.

In Stonesbury, the Charter Committee grew stronger every day. At the end of the month, Nathaniel called for a public meeting. "There will be no meeting unless the town council calls it," Rockmore announced. But that didn't stop Nathaniel and the Charter Committee.

Samuel understood why the town leaders were worried. If the Charter Committee got its way, the Puritan church would lose its hold over Stonesbury. Samuel agreed with the Puritans that God's law was higher than the King's. But he didn't agree that the Puritans were the only ones who could know God's law. Under the new charter, men of all religions would help shape town laws. To Samuel, that only seemed right.

One week before the public charter meeting, Samuel sat at his workbench. His master was away at a meeting of church elders. The whole town seemed to twitch with nervousness. But in spite of Rockmore's repeated warnings, Nathaniel and his men were not backing down.

Samuel began cutting out the soles for a pair of shoes. He was so deep in thought that he did not notice Anne Rockmore slip in the door. She stood pressed to the wall where she would be out of sight from passers-by.

"Samuel," she whispered.

He jumped, and almost made a bad cut in the cowhide.

"I'm sorry," Anne said, still whispering. "I wanted to talk to you. I know that Father and Uncle are in a meeting this morning. So I thought we might have a moment."

"Look," Samuel began. "I've got to work. Please go immediately." He knew he could afford no more mistakes. Being alone with the Reverend's daughter certainly would be one.

"My father says you are a Quaker."

"And what of it?" Samuel asked cautiously.

"He is afraid that you are with the men who want the new charter. He says you will start a Quaker church in Stonesbury."

Samuel laughed harshly. "If you are asking if there is truth in that, no, there is not. I think your father should stop worrying so much about the lives of others."

"Yes," Anne said quietly. "But I've come to warn you. I know that Father caught you sneaking out the other night."

"A man cannot go to the outhouse at night?"

"Oh, Samuel, you just don't understand the ways of our people. Strange behavior can be a death sentence. My father says you were out that night to seek entrance into the souls of sleeping people.

"I have heard my uncle defend you time and again," Anne went on. "He knows you to be a good man. But he can speak up for you only so long. You know what has happened to the people who have spoken for the accused in Salem."

"I'm not sure what you are saying," Samuel said. "I've committed no crime. Why do you mention Salem?"

Perhaps you should stay home at night," Anne said, ignoring the question. "And—

above all—don't go to the charter meeting next week."

"I am not afraid of your father."

"Oh, Samuel, don't be foolish."

Samuel looked closely at Anne. "Why are you so concerned for me?"

Anne paused and flushed a deep red. "I've watched you come and go from that window many a night . . . ," she began and then stopped.

Samuel was suddenly struck by how different she was from Susannah. Anne often had a fresh look, as if she'd just been doing hard work. She looked very beautiful.

"I must go," she said. "But first, may I borrow that book you've been reading?" Now she smiled playfully.

"First you order me to be careful in the smallest of details. Then you ask me to lend the leading preacher's daughter a book he thinks evil. I already told you, no!"

"There's no law against reading, Samuel."

"Then ask your father for books."

"Ah, he believes that all books except the Bible are evil."

"Most of the things Nathaniel and I read are political or philosophical," Samuel said. "I don't know that they would interest you."

"Oh, they would!" Anne said, brushing the hair out of her face. When she smiled at him, Samuel could not help smiling back.

"Be gone," he said, suddenly aware of how long their conversation had lasted. "Before the town council returns from its meeting."

"Do bring me something to read some time," she called as she left. As the door closed behind her, Samuel realized that he was very much in love.

The following Monday the town council held another meeting. Samuel put the muddy Locke book inside his jacket and left the shop. He crossed the street to the well. From there he darted behind the blacksmith's shop and, in plain sight, across the field. "I must be possessed!" Samuel thought. For he felt driven by a power outside of himself. He had to see Anne.

Samuel stopped on the edge of the woods behind Rockmore's house. What luck! There she was, carrying a bucket of water from the well to the pumpkin patch. Samuel watched her for a minute. His heart thundered in his chest. Then he cupped his hands over his mouth and made a quiet birdcall.

When she looked up he motioned for her to come toward him. A smile burst across Anne's face, but she turned her back to him. She returned the bucket to the well. Then she gathered her apron in her hands as if she were going to hunt for greens. Only then did Anne head toward the woods.

"Oh, Samuel!" she cried as he grabbed her hands. "I'm so glad to see you." But her smile disappeared quickly.

"What is the matter, Anne?"

"It's Father. He's taking this witch business so seriously."

"Well, no one has been hanged yet," Samuel said.

"Yet," Anne repeated, shaking her head. "I know one is supposed to respect one's father. But I believe mine has gone quite mad. And, he is leading others into madness."

"It is true that the people seem to hang on his every word." Samuel winced at his own choice of words. "But, listen. We haven't much time." Samuel wanted to change the subject. "I've brought you something." He held up the book by John Locke.

"You changed your mind!" Anne said, and laughed. "Thank you. Perhaps this will keep my mind off other things."

"Actually, it was an excuse to come see you," Samuel said. "But I am out of place for saying so," he added, thinking of his upcoming marriage.

"I suppose you are," Anne replied. "But I am still glad to see you." She put her hands on his shoulders, and kissed his cheek. Then, with the book in her apron, Anne hurried back to the garden.

The Charter Meeting

On the evening of the charter meeting, the men of Stonesbury gathered in the commons after supper. Samuel returned to the shop, even though business was slow now. With the beginning of warm, dry weather, most people put their shoes away. So Samuel busied himself by cleaning and sharpening tools for Saturday's house-raising.

Being the biggest man in town, Samuel was always popular at house-raisings. Even so, he knew Johnson Bains never would have invited him if he weren't Bacon's apprentice. Bains was a church elder and a town council member. And he was one of Rockmore's strongest supporters.

Samuel looked forward to the house-raising. Anne would be within sight all day. Even better, he might find a way the two of them could have a moment alone.

At dusk Samuel put away the cleaned and sharpened tools. He stepped outside and locked the shop. The air felt thick. The sky had turned a dark, stormy gray.

Samuel looked across the commons to the meetinghouse. Through the waxed paper windows, he saw the dim light of wall candles. He heard men's voices, already raised in anger.

Before he knew it, Samuel crossed the commons and slipped in the back of the packed meetinghouse.

"You have no right to preside over this meeting!" a farmer shouted at the council. "The men who called the meeting should run it."

"We are the town council," thundered Rockmore. "When there is a meeting in this town, we preside."

"To continue with business," Nathaniel shouted, ignoring Rockmore. "I will now explain the purpose of this meeting—"

"Silence!" ordered Rockmore. "You are not a voting member of this town. You may not speak."

"It is his *right!*" The blacksmith stood and pointed his finger at Rockmore. He was one of the few church members who supported the King's new charter. "The new charter states that freeholders of any faith shall have the right to vote. And that also means the right to voice opinions in town meetings."

Rockmore's face turned brick red. "You shall be punished for taking the Devil's side," he told the blacksmith. "This is God's town, not the King's."

Soon all the members of the town council were standing. A dozen other men stood facing them. Everyone shouted at once. More and more men rose to their feet. A few began to push toward the front and the council. Samuel heard Nathaniel scream, "Stay seated! No fighting! Stay seated!" The meetinghouse seemed ready to explode in anger.

Samuel could stand it no more. He stood and shouted, "Listen!" His height and deep voice silenced the room. Everyone turned to look at him.

Avoiding his master's eyes, Samuel spoke. "It is true this is God's town. It is God's country, too. And God's Earth. But God alone cannot see to it that men do not murder their fellow citizens as they are doing in Salem. God alone cannot make sure that one man's fields are not grazed by another man's cows. Surely God expects us to use His guidance to govern ourselves. Men make laws. Yes, even in Stonesbury, you know that men make the laws. We should be guided by God. But God speaks to each of us in His own way. I say, every man a vote!"

A roar of applause rose up in the meetinghouse. "Here! Here!" a chorus of men cried. "Listen to Samuel Roberts." The men began stomping their feet and chanting, "Every man a vote! Every man a vote!"

Then suddenly a rumbling outside stirred the night. A crack of lightning lit the room. Thunder shook the meetinghouse. Then several more jags of lightning struck close by.

The men pushed and shoved to get to the door. No one doubted that God Himself had spoken. And no one missed Rockmore's roar sounding above the storm. "It is the work of the Devil's helper!" he yelled.

Stunned by his own brilliant foolishness, Samuel didn't move. The Puritans made a wide circle in rushing by him. A small group, including the blacksmith and Nathaniel, slapped Samuel on the back.

"Well spoken," Nathaniel said. "Bad luck on the timing of that storm." Then they hurried past.

Finally Samuel left the empty meeting-house alone. He walked back across the commons, getting soaked by the sudden storm. At the door to the cobbler's shop Samuel hesitated, and then entered. The master stood warming his hands at the fire, his back turned to the door.

"That you, Samuel?"

"Yes, sir."

Master Bacon turned around. Samuel expected to see an angry face looking back at him. Instead, Bacon looked sad. "Young man, you have grown up a lot since you dragged yourself into Stonesbury four years ago."

"Yes, sir."

"You've proven to be an excellent apprentice. Skilled, honest, hard-working. I could not have asked for more if you were my own son. That is why I offered you partnership and marriage to Susannah."

The master paused, so Samuel said, "Yes, sir."

"I daresay I acted too soon," Bacon went on. "I will be generous and say that perhaps your problem is youth. You've become a man and you want to make your mark. Well, I can understand that. *But in good time, my boy!* Why do you throw yourself in with these rebels?" Bacon leaned against the hearth, waiting for an answer.

"I don't believe they are rebels, sir. Almost half the town believes as they—as we—do. Sir, it's only fair that people should vote in town affairs. If I had my way, *all* men would vote. Whether they owned property or not."

Bacon's face tightened in anger as he straightened up and began pacing.

"My boy, you are misguided. For what reason would someone without property have a need to vote? Ah, don't answer. Let me get to my point. I believe you'll grow out of all this. I *urge* you to grow out of it, and soon. What do you have to gain? In a few short months, if all goes well, you will own property. Therefore you need simply to join the church. Then you will be a voting member of this town.

"And if, as a voter, you wish to change the ways of this town, that will be your right. I shall not stand in your way. I daresay you have a better head on your shoulders than many that lead Stonesbury now. Certainly by speaking up when you did tonight, you prevented a sure brawl. I see that. But you are young. You must learn to follow the rules, son."

Bacon continued to pace, his face furrowed in a deep frown. "I'll say no more. I am going to forget what happened tonight. Though I am sure my brother-in-law will not. In one month, I am going to make your marriage and our partnership public. Your conversion to the Puritan church should occur well before then. Do you understand?"

Samuel nodded silently.

Without further comment, Master Bacon then quickly left the shop. Samuel stayed and worked several more hours by candlelight. His mind raced over the events of the last few weeks. He tried to reason with himself. He tried to put his stubbornness aside.

But his master's warning only lodged Samuel's beliefs more tightly in his head. Every man had a right to his say in town government. Every man had a right to his own religious beliefs. Samuel knew these to be truths.

On the other hand, his master was right. If he simply converted to the Puritan church and married Susannah, he would have everything. Then he could speak out whenever he pleased. He would be in a good position to make some real changes in this town. Samuel was torn between his two choices.

The following day, however, Samuel discovered that he was in grave trouble. The sky was clear and blue. The storm, which struck just as he spoke last night, had left just as suddenly. The Puritans took this to be a sure sign that Samuel Roberts was Satan's soldier.

Women yanked children to their sides as Samuel passed them on the street. Others leaned out of windows to watch him pass, as if he were a circus sideshow.

That afternoon, Anne Rockmore stepped into the shop. She did not give Samuel so much as a glance. Instead she said to Master Bacon, "Father asked me to come speak to you. He has called a town council meeting for three o'clock."

"Thank you, niece," Bacon answered without looking up from a nearly finished shoe.

Then looking directly at Samuel, Ann repeated, "At *three*."

"Yes, I heard you." Bacon looked up.

"I wasn't sure," Anne answered, and left.

At three o'clock Master Bacon left the shop. Samuel waited ten minutes and then stood up. He sat back down. Then stood again. He just couldn't reason with himself. He knew Anne expected him to meet her in the garden.

"Well," Samuel said. "If I am going to hang, I may as well see her one last time."

Boldly, as if he were doing nothing more than going to the store, Samuel crossed the commons. He made his way to the woods behind Rockmore's house. His heart jumped at the sight of Anne. He wanted to grab her up and run far away.

As if she had read his thoughts, the first thing Anne said was, "Run away with me. Let's go to Philadelphia. Let's go anywhere but Stonesbury. Please, Samuel."

"You know we can't do that." Samuel put on his most responsible voice. His words betrayed his true feelings.

Anne shook him by the elbow. "Don't you know Father believes you are a witch? Don't you know that after last night, the whole town thinks so as well?"

"Not the whole town. A lot of people here have more sense than that."

"Yes, but the ones in power are the ones that count. Your master is the only town council member who will stand up for you. How long do you think he can do that? You must *do* something."

Samuel leaned against a pear tree on the edge of the forest. He thought his heart would break. The only thing that would save him now was conversion to the Puritan church. And marriage to Susannah.

"Anne, you know I am to be married in a few months. I cannot run out on my responsibility, my obligation."

"Oh!" Anne cried, folding her arms in a fury. "Those are big words, indeed!"

"Anne, can't you understand?"

"No, I can't. Your responsibility and obligation to *whom*? What about your own beliefs and feelings? Don't they count for anything? You will publicly convert so that you can marry Susannah and gain oh, so much property. Perhaps you did not read your Locke well enough. What about each man's right to life and liberty? What about religious liberty?"

"Oh ho!" Now Samuel was angry, too. "So you have some big words to use yourself! You may forget that Locke also says each man has the right to own possessions—"

"It is a question of what comes first. You would sell your own happiness, and your very thoughts, for the right to own possessions? I'm not sure Locke would admire that!"

"Look, Anne, forget Locke. I came to Stonesbury without a penny to my name. I've served four hardworking years as an apprentice. And I am not going to give that up to have nothing again. What kind of life would we have if we ran away? Maybe we could scratch out a living on some stony farm somewhere.

"You know, I think you have your own reasons for wanting to run away with me," Samuel continued. "You want to use me to escape your father. Isn't that what you really want, Anne? This has little to do with me. You want out—out of that house, and out of Stonesbury. And you think I might be able to help you."

"You can't believe that," she whispered. "Samuel, I'd give up just what you would. Don't you know that Father will find me a wealthy man to marry? I would inherit the most luxurious life there is to be had in Stonesbury. But to me it is not worth it. I love *you*. Not some rich church member I don't know."

"Yes, Anne." Samuel took her in his arms. "I love you, too. But here's the truth of it. Even if I had the money to buy a small piece of land, I don't know how to farm. You must understand, I am *penniless*. We would have to sleep in the woods, eat berries and roots. I will not take you into that kind of life."

"There must be a way," Anne said, holding back her tears. "There must be."

"You are more stubborn than I," Samuel said, smiling sadly. "I must go. Master Bacon expects me to have finished the shoes I am working on by the time he returns."

"Ah, responsibility again," Anne said angrily. She turned and strode across the garden and went back into the house.

The House-Raising

"My fellow townspeople," Samuel began. "Thank you for coming this evening to hear my deepest feelings. There has been a change in my life, an enormous change. I have been lost in a sea of doubt. I was cast here and there by the beliefs of others." Samuel bowed his head, and looked sorrowful. His eyes begged forgiveness.

"My soul was an open door. It is little surprise that the Devil made his entry so easily. I've asked you here today to tell you I have fought him off. I am happy to announce that my prayers brought change. I would like to ask the church elders to admit me to the Puritan church whose beliefs—"

"I can't!" Samuel kicked at a fern on the ground. He looked at his audience, a stand of sugar pines in the woods behind the shoemaker's house. "I'm sorry, I just can't do it."

He sank down and sat on some moss at the base of a tree. He closed his eyes and remembered the trip to America eight years before. He had stood on the deck of the ship, the salty ocean wind blowing in his face.

"Samuel, we are leaving England and going to America," his mother had said then. "We will have no property. But we will be together. And we will have God in our hearts to guide us."

Samuel's parents had given up everything they had for what they believed in. He could not sacrifice *his* beliefs now. Not just for the sake of property and a comfortable life. If he did, he felt as if he would be betraying them.

Samuel decided he would go to the house-raising on Saturday. There he would find a way, somehow, to say goodbye to Anne. Then Saturday night, he'd take to the road. He didn't know where he would go. But he knew he had to leave Stonesbury.

"Well?" Master Bacon asked when Samuel returned to the shop. He'd given Samuel the morning off to practice his conversion speech.

"I'm not quite ready, sir," Samuel said.

Bacon looked at him sternly. "It would be much better if you did it before the house-raising on Saturday. I promised the Reverend Rockmore that it would be *soon*. After your performance at the charter meeting the other night . . ."

"I know, sir, but I need to work out a few more things."

"It doesn't have to be long, my boy. Repent and say you would like to join the church."

"Yes, sir. I'll be ready Sunday."

"All right," Bacon said shaking his head. "Sunday then. They'll need your strength at the house-raising anyway. I doubt anyone will object to your presence."

As it turned out, however, Bacon was wrong. On Saturday, as he and Samuel arrived at the house-raising, the churchmen called a meeting.

"Let him touch your house and it will crumble tonight!" one man cried.

Another lowered his voice and said, "But he does the work of ten men. Isn't it better to overlook his shortcomings for today?"

Disgusted, Samuel stood to the side as the men discussed their problem. He looked over the cleared field. On the ground lay the timbers that Bains had already felled and squared. Some were fastened together for the broadsides. The rafter beams were stacked nearby. A neat pile of treenails lay near the chimney which was already in place.

"A house built with the hands of the Devil will not stand a year," proclaimed the Reverend Rockmore. But finally, even he was reluctant to send Samuel home. The job would be done that much sooner with his help.

Suddenly Samuel was filled with anger. He stepped around the group of men. He took hold of one broadside. And, with anger fueling his strength, Samuel began hefting it all by himself. The rest of the men looked on, amazed.

Finally, Bains himself said, "But he's as strong as an ox." So the men shrugged and joined Samuel in the work.

After the broadsides were raised, a group of men steadied them. Two other groups raised the end girts. Bains began to drive in treenails to hold the beams in place.

"Lunch time," Rockmore announced.

"Shouldn't Bains finish pinning the frame first?" Samuel asked. The other men knew he should. But since Samuel seemed to be challenging Rockmore, no one dared to agree out loud.

Samuel pressed his point. "Without at least a few more treenails, a wind could blow this over." When no one answered, Samuel followed the group to the tables of food.

The women had spread a huge lunch of pies and roasted meats. As he ate, Samuel looked at Anne as often as he dared. He had to find a way to see her alone for a second.

Then, after lunch, his chance came. The whole group left the lunch tables to go inspect Bain's spring. As they were leaving, Samuel caught Anne's eye. He jerked his head toward a stand of white pines. Without anyone noticing, both he and Anne slipped in back of the trees.

"I'm leaving tonight, Anne," he told her. "I have realized you are right. I cannot go against my own beliefs. Nor can I marry against my feelings. The only choice I have is to leave Massachusetts at once—and never come back."

"No!" Anne shook her head back and forth. "What about us?"

"You know I have no way of making a living. And even if I did, your father would never allow us to marry."

"Where's Samuel Roberts?" someone shouted. "Has anyone seen Samuel Roberts? It's time to raise the rafters."

"Quick," Samuel said, taking Anne into his arms. "There is no time. But I had to say goodbye."

"Someone find Roberts!" a voice bellowed again. It was Rockmore.

"No, Samuel, you can't go!" Anne took his face in her hands.

Samuel closed his eyes and kissed Anne. For one final moment, they held each other tightly. Then, one more kiss—

The Reverend Rockmore crashed through the trees and stood before the couple. "Father!" Anne cried. Rockmore's eyes were daggers of hatred. He seized Samuel by the front of his jacket. Then he pulled him out from behind the trees into plain sight.

"Take him to prison!" ordered the Reverend. A group of men surrounded Samuel. They dragged him to the nearest wagon.

Then, like thunder from the sky, came Rockmore's voice. "Oh, Satan has come to Stonesbury, at last!"

Samuel, and everyone else, looked up. Rockmore had climbed onto the newly erected frame of the house. His arms were outstretched and his head was thrown back. The Reverend Rockmore loved preaching from heights.

"Reverend Rockmore!" Samuel shouted. "The frame hasn't been properly pinned!"

The men wrestled Samuel to the ground as if he had cursed Rockmore.

Rockmore began preaching. "This witch shall be tried to the fullest of God's law. We shall weed out the Devil's poison from Stonesbury! We shall . . ."

The timber beneath Rockmore's feet trembled. "Tell him," Samuel mumbled into the hands pressed over his mouth. "Tell him to get down."

But no one moved. Everyone seemed to be frozen in the confusion of the moment. Rockmore preached louder and louder. The entire frame of the house began shaking. Samuel could only watch in horror.

Finally, Rockmore noticed the frame moving beneath him. He stopped preaching and reached for something to hold on to. But he was seconds too late. One broadside began slowly falling away. Rockmore thrashed about for something to grab. But there was nothing. In an instant he fell to the ground. A moment later the second broadside came crashing down on top of him. The Reverend Rockmore was crushed to death.

CHAPTER 8

Powers of Darkness on Trial

Samuel felt a hard slap across his face. Then another. He opened his eyes. He found himself slumped on the floor of the meeting-house. Then he remembered that he had passed out at the beginning of his own trial.

"Can the prisoner take the stand?"

Samuel recognized his master's voice. Bacon was in command of the town council now that his brother-in-law was dead. "Yes," answered Samuel.

"Then do so."

Samuel was placed in a chair before the council, whose members sat at one long table.

"We have before us Samuel Roberts, 20 years old. He is on trial for witchcraft and the

murder of the Reverend Rockmore,"
announced Simon Weatherby, the town crier.

"Murder?" Samuel said. "I was nowhere
near Rockmore or the house when it fell!"

"Witches needn't use their own hands to
do evil. They send their deeds through Devil
spirits," answered Simon.

Samuel desperately looked to Bacon for
guidance. "Master, sir! Surely you don't
believe this! Surely—" Samuel could not find
the right words. Master Bacon remained
silent, his face a blank mask.

Samuel searched the faces of the other
town council members. Simon Weatherby,
Johnson Bains, and the other two men stared
back boldly.

Just then Samuel heard the sound of a
galloping horse pounding up the cobblestones
outside. The doors of the meetinghouse flew
open. Nathaniel burst in the room. Sweat
poured from his face as he gasped for air.
Nathaniel waved a roll of paper in the air.

"I must interrupt the trial," he shouted,
still out of breath. "I have come fresh from
Boston with important news."

Before anyone could stop him, Nathaniel continued. "I have in my hand a copy of the King's new charter. The Royal Governor's own scribe copied it this past night. You may read for yourselves about our right to a vote in town matters. Not only that, I've alerted officials in Boston. Should Stonesbury ignore the King's orders, the Royal Governor himself shall come to town.

"Therefore," Nathaniel went on, "I demand that the law be put into practice immediately. I believe that Samuel Roberts is innocent on all counts. Can we take a vote on that?"

Nathaniel stepped forward and placed the charter before Bacon. "I beseech you, sir. You are now head of the town council. Please give this a fair read."

Bacon took the charter in his shaking hands. It seemed to Samuel that hours passed as Bacon studied the document.

Though his face showed nothing, Bacon was very troubled. How could he hang this young man he had grown to love? In his heart he knew all too well that Samuel was no witch. He also knew that Samuel had nothing to do with Rockmore's death. Yet some of Rockmore's supporters were so dedicated that they had already built a gallows.

Five, and then ten minutes passed. Surely by now, Bacon thought, everyone was disgusted by how weak-willed he was. He *had* to make a decision.

Then it dawned on him. Everyone in the room was waiting in silence for his reply. Indeed, there was a great deal of power in leadership. He need only take it.

So Bacon came up with his plan. He was pleased with his own cleverness. He just hoped the town accepted it.

"It must be the will of God," Bacon finally announced. "Why else would the charter be brought before me? So we shall have a town vote. All those in favor of freeing Samuel Roberts from charges of witchcraft and murder, say 'aye.'"

For several moments a deathly silence hung in the air. Weatherby, Bains, and the others leaned forward to scowl at Bacon. But Bacon fixed his gaze straight ahead. He sat as tall as a king.

Then Nathaniel's "aye" rang out. Another one followed. Then a chorus of "ayes" fell on Samuel's head like so many gold coins.

Bacon nodded and called out, "All opposed, say 'nay.'"

This time there was no hesitation. A roar of "nays" filled the room. Samuel's eyes locked with Bacon's. He saw then that Bacon wished for Samuel's life almost as much as Samuel did.

"We shall have a hand vote, then," Bacon said, his voice trembling.

"What do you mean, a hand vote?" shouted Johnson Bains. "The 'nays' were far louder. I say hang Roberts!"

Bacon ignored Bains. Instead he called for, and then counted, hands. Samuel studied the floor. He could not bear to watch.

"So be it!" cried Bacon, unable to hide his joy. "Two hundred and thirty-one 'ayes.' Two hundred and thirty 'nays.' The prisoner is free!"

A cheer of relief swept the crowd. Tears ran freely down Samuel's face.

Bacon felt a surge of well-being. *He* was in charge now. He held up his hand to keep order in the meetinghouse. "I would like to say a few words," he said. When people quieted, he went on. "I am only now beginning to realize what has come over New England in these past months. How close we of Stonesbury have come to the madness of Salem. We have become a colony gripped by fear. Let us thank God we have not taken the final step the people of Salem have.

"Stonesbury is not a big town. Yet it is big enough for all of us. I have lived and worked with young Samuel Roberts for four years. I know him to be as fine a citizen as there is in our town. In good faith, I would like to announce that Samuel Roberts shall become my partner in business. And, he shall marry my daughter Susannah."

A chorus of disapproving gasps rippled through the meetinghouse. The others on the town council seethed in anger. But Bacon rocked back in his chair. He folded his hands over his belly and smiled.

"Sir?" called Nathaniel. "May I speak?"

"I suppose so."

"Sir, I would like to thank you for speaking so wisely," Nathaniel said nervously.

"However, it is my wish that *I* might marry your daughter Susannah. I love her, and I do believe she loves me."

"What!" Bacon came to his feet and stared in shock at Nathaniel.

"It is my wish, too, Father," Susannah said from the back of the meetinghouse. Samuel whipped his head around to stare at her. Then he remembered Nathaniel's strange looks whenever Susannah's name had come up between them. Everything suddenly fell into place.

"You are now the guardian of your niece," continued Nathaniel. "It is her wish to marry Samuel Roberts. And I believe that it is his to marry her."

"Young man, you are too bold," Bacon cautioned in a stern voice.

"Yes, sir, I am. But this plan serves the happiness of everyone."

Bacon looked out over the sea of astonished faces. The building itself seemed to hold its breath. To be sure, a new age was dawning on Stonesbury.

"Well," he said, almost as if he were thinking aloud. "It is true that I am now Anne

Rockmore's guardian. That gives me one more girl I must marry off. And one more dowry to pay. If I can marry two girls with this plan, I should find it acceptable."

"Still, I shall need Samuel in the shop. As Anne is now my daughter, really, her dowry shall be the same as Susannah's. That leaves much less for Susannah's dowry."

"I have the store, sir," Nathaniel said. "I have no need for a dowry."

Bacon shook his head, stunned. But he couldn't help being well pleased with Nathaniel's offer. "This is hardly town business," he said, unable to hold in a laugh.

"Yes, it is!" shouted the blacksmith. "All in favor of these two marriages say, 'aye!'"

A long-needed merriment washed over the people of Stonesbury. Even some of the sternest of the Puritans were laughing. Samuel couldn't believe his ears.

"Attention! Attention!" Bacon hammered the table to get order. He put on his sternest face. "Still I must sentence Samuel Roberts. He has kissed a woman who is not his wife. For that he should spend two days in the pillory."

"But sir," Simon Weatherby said. Even he cracked a smile. "Anne Rockmore is already in the pillory for kissing Roberts!"

"Then move her to the stocks."

"Long live the King!" shouted Nathaniel.

"Long live the King!" many others answered.

As the townspeople filed out of the meetinghouse, Nathaniel pushed his way over to Samuel. The two young men embraced. Then Samuel looked at his friend with tears in his eyes.

"You saved my life, Nathaniel," Samuel said. "I can find no words to thank you."

Nathaniel smiled warmly. "I know you would have done the same for me, Samuel," he said. "There is a new feeling in Stonesbury now," Nathaniel added. "A feeling of freedom. And we can use that feeling to make things different. Stonesbury can become one of the best places to live in all the colonies."

"Yes," Samuel agreed smiling. And together they walked through the crowd and into the bright morning sunshine.